Ladybird

This Little Story
belongs to

_____

Published by Ladybird Books Ltd
27 Wrights Lane London W8 5TZ
A Penguin Company
3 5 7 9 10 8 6 4 2

Printed in Italy

Little
Lost Puppy

by Ronne Randall
illustrated by Karen Hiscock

Little Puppy and Bunny were best friends.

Every day they played tag, and chase-the-ball, and who-can-jump-higher, and hide-and-seek.

They had so much fun together!

Then one day Bunny moved away to a new home.

Little Puppy was sad and missed his friend. But then he realised that he could visit Bunny, and they could play together as they always did.

Bunny's new home was far away.
So Little Puppy made up a special
rhyme to help him remember how
to get there:

"Down the lane
And past the mill,
Turn right at the big tree
Over the hill…

Past the field
Where the horses play –
I'm off to see Bunny
And I know the way!"

Where are you going, Little Puppy?

I'm off to see my friend, Bunny!

Bunny was always happy to see his friend. And Little Puppy was happy to be there. But sometimes he felt just a little worried.

"What if I forget the way next time I come?" he asked Bunny. "Or what if I get lost going home?"

"You don't need to worry," Bunny
told him. "If you get lost, just go
back the way you came! All you
have to do is to think of this rhyme:

"If you lose your way,
Don't be downhearted –
Just follow your steps
Back to where you started!"

One night, there was a loud and blustery storm. The wind howled and moaned and shook the branches of the trees. Little Puppy couldn't sleep.

"I hope I'll be able to visit Bunny tomorrow," he thought.

By next morning the storm was over. The air was calm and clear, and the sun was shining.

"I *will* be able to visit Bunny today," thought Little Puppy happily.

As he set off, Little Puppy noticed
big heaps of leaves in the lane.
"The storm must have blown
them from the trees last night,"
he thought.

Little Puppy jumped and danced
through the leaves. "This is fun!"
he laughed, kicking them high into
the air.

As he went along, Little Puppy said his rhyme to himself:

> "Down the lane
> And past the mill,
> Turn right at the big tree
> Over the hill!"

He clambered happily over the hill as he always did, and scurried down the other side.

Suddenly Little Puppy stopped. Where was the big tree? He couldn't see it anywhere!

Little Puppy was so confused that he didn't know which way to turn. He ran down the lane, trying to remember the rest of the way to Bunny's house.

"Past the field where the horses play," he said to himself. *"That is the way to Bunny's today!"*

But Little Puppy didn't see the field where the friendly horses played. Instead he saw a mossy stone wall and an old barn.

"I can't remember seeing *this* on the way to Bunny's house," he thought as he passed by.

Little Puppy went on, and after a while he did come to a field.

"*This* must be where the horses play!" he said to himself. But it wasn't. There were no horses in this field, just a raggedy old scarecrow.

"I can't remember seeing *this* on the way to Bunny's house!" said Little Puppy. He was *very* worried now. In fact, he felt like crying.

Then Little Puppy remembered
what Bunny had told him:

'If you lose your way,
don't be downhearted –
Just follow your steps
Back to where you started!'

"*That's* what I need to do," thought
Little Puppy. "I'll go back the way
I came!"

Back Little Puppy went,
  past the scarecrow…
    past the old barn…
      and past the mossy wall.

At last Little Puppy found himself
back at the bottom of the hill.

"I know where I am now," he said
happily. "And there's the big tree.
It must have blown over in the storm
last night!"

Little Puppy leapt over the tree trunk, and scampered merrily down the lane. Before he knew it he could see his friends the horses.

"*Here's* the field where the horses play," he said. "*This* is the way to Bunny's today!"

And so Little Puppy found his way
to Bunny's home at last.

"Oh, I'm so glad to see you!"
Bunny exclaimed. "I was worried—
I thought you might have got lost!"

"I did get lost," said Little Puppy.

"Then how did you get here?"
asked Bunny.

"I did exactly what you told me to," said Little Puppy. "Although I was lost, I wasn't downhearted – I just followed my steps back to where I started!"

"You went back the way you came!" said Bunny.

"Yes," said Little Puppy. "And now that I know how to do that, I'll never worry about getting lost again!"

And off they went for a lively game of tag.